PETTY DOESN'T PAY

Written by
Jacob Grovey

Illustrated by
Michael Okoroagha

Thank You

"Petty Doesn't Pay," but kindness goes a long way. The release of this book was made possible by the generosity of several people who believed in the work.

Your donations mean the world to me!

Edie Phillips

Shaluan Douglas

Clint & Nikki Fludd

Eldred White

Allison Haviland

Artasia Harris

Curtiss Atwater

Eugenia McNaron

Chaundra Rickerson

Marcus Jones

Nekia Tharps-Becerra

Chandra Hill

Mia Edwards

Rebecca Acosta

Darryl Johnson

Matthew E. Smith

Deloris Grovey Williams

Chris House

Jamar Jefferson

Tamica Jackson

Ronald Bell

Miles Guilette

Madeline Wilkerson

Angela Jacobs-Butler

Tonya Williams-Hardin

Amber Satchell

Rebeca Perales

Christine St. Laurent

Angela Govan

Carolyn Jacobs

Levi Chaney

Devin Randon

Johann Jacobs

Jermaine Joseph

We deal with petty people almost every single day, but I'm here to tell you, petty doesn't pay.

You start your day by giving thanks and praises for being alive.

Then, your vibe is instantly shot when you get cut off by that person who doesn't know how to drive.

u try to shake it off by getting some coffee from that place with the nice ambiance and

ol lights, but that person who acted like they didn't see you in line, almost made

u want to fight.

You take a deep breath because you're trying not to curse, and then it was almost like that barista's mission was to make things worse. He tried to give you a single mocha when you paid for a double, but that's not even the part that almost got him into trouble.

Your name is very easy to spell, but he decided he wanted to make it better.

So when you finally got your coffee cup, it had all kinds of unnecessary letters.

This was your breaking point, so you threw your $8 coffee on the floor. I guess you wanted to waste money and pretend you didn't need caffeine anymore.

They didn't have the greatest service, but you weren't a great customer, either.

When it comes to being petty, we tend to follow others, instead of being leaders.

When you got to work, you saw tons of messages requesting reports you had already turned in. I guess your supervisor didn't check their inbox before they decided to press send.

You realized pettiness seems all too common with people of power. I mean, just look at the news on any day, at any given hour.

On social media, presidents, senators, and other politicians are sending messages of hate, but it would be petty of me to question how that will make America great.

The outside world is full of people who seem to be on a mission to annoy.

Believe it or not, our friends and family can also be the ones who try to take away our joy.

Everyone plays a role in being petty, but let me make things a little clearer,

the world's petty population begins with the person in the mirror.

We all have something to achieve, so we can't let a petty person stop it.

Everything works for our good, I mean, even this book's writer is using petty to make a profit.

I guess in that way, petty does pay,

but we all must ask ourselves, "Why am I being so petty today?"